DOOR = JAR

Door Is A Jar
Issue 23

www.doorisajarmagazine.net

Editors

Maxwell Bauman, Editor-in-Chief/ Art Director

Jack Fabian, Managing Editor/ Nonfiction Editor

Nina Long, Fiction Editor

Corrine Nulton, Poetry Editor/ Drama Editor

Cover Image "Bad Apples"
by Karen Boissonneault-Gauthier

Table of Contents

Hiking 2
Jeffery Letterly
Poetry

The DCR pamphlet on hiker safety tips insists
on layers and bringing essentials, warns
against confronting wildlife and wandering
off the blazed trail. But there are other things
that are left unaddressed — how do you tell yourself
to keep going when calves ache
only after a half mile? What do you do
if every tree reminds you of the work
you left behind, the car inspection you keep
forgetting to schedule, the panicked feeling
when you got lost in a department store
at the age of six and couldn't see
over the conglomeration of circular clothing racks?
If there's a lightning storm, avoid open water.
Avoid high ground. Avoid open spaces.
Keep your distance from other people—
you should be doing that anyway — love
and attraction can be the most dangerous.
Adequate preparation is necessary
for a safe experience.

Anxiety
Brontë Pearson
Poetry

I am an ever-inflating balloon
stretching wider and thinner
from a steady stream of unapologetic air
bursting through the weak curtains of my lips

A cyclonic pressure with no respect
And I can't exhale against this force
so my heart thumps like a heavy stone
that leaves gashes and bruises in my chest
and I anticipate my death before I rupture

An obituary of suffering without action

But the combustion never comes
and my skin becomes so malleable
yet I cannot shake such malefic worry
with every bit of me filled so uncomfortably

Heartache
Brontë Pearson
Poetry

My chest is full of wet muslin cloths,
a sopping heap of something light
turned heavier than expected,
and it's all because my mind
connected words that did not mean
what I thought they did, and so
I disappointed myself by longing
for a dream that was never real
because I miss the past
and bleed in the present
and want a future that can clot
my wounds the way I want them,
but how can I seek control when
I can't even tame my own sadness?

Just One Tear
Brontë Pearson
Poetry

The seeping sad globe
is cold on my porous sheath
like a chilled fingertip
sliding across wrapping paper,
smooth but catching on wild terrain,
a world of excess —
feeling contained but uncontainable —
slowly slithering until gravity consumes
it like a hungry phagocyte,
almost as if my universe
was never overflowing.

Never Trust a Salesman
Brontë Pearson
Poetry

He'll sell you love with a promise
that your friendship was a sturdy
foundation despite the empty years
and that the girl who broke his heart
faded at the sight of you and all
your admirable light that made
accepting your chaos worthwhile
and he'll stitch himself into the parts
of you that you hide from the world
and let your sheltered blood percolate
at your inviting seams for him
to lap it up with a hungry tongue
until you are drained of all he needs
and he'll kiss you goodbye one last time
and tell you that he just wasn't ready
for everything you had to offer.

Ambient
Robert Beveridge
Poetry

Your body silhouetted in blue glow.
Wisp of blouse transparent, curves
in outline. One fingernail traces
the boundary of your bra, considers
the lack of matched set below. To kiss
your shoulder, your throat! You dance
away, sidestep without motion.
Ribs compress, constrict, tightened
muscles beg a drop of rain
from the Patagonian desert.
Moistened, they demand the contents
of flood plains. To kiss your lips,
read erotic novels with your eyes.
To be light.

Audition
Robert Beveridge
Poetry

Eyes front, back arched, no sign
you are aware the rows of seats
go back, and back, and back
further than you have ever seen.
Leg up, hands thrust into the space
between the worlds. Your mouth
forms the words, but your mind
discusses with itself whether you
are low on Kona, if you will make
it to your next appointment, how
many lionesses can dance on the head
of John the Baptist (both before
and after removal). Your clothes
disheveled, but your coiffure pristine.

Vocal
Robert Beveridge
Poetry

Smoke and gravel, mixed,
the room's atmosphere
and the smell of sandalwood
incense, tobacco, pine.
Coffee with cream. Taste
of tongue, saliva,
foreign language with a hint
of lime. The sweet grip,
the pull of citrus.

When The White Horse Takes Me Away
Robert Beveridge
Poetry

the honeybees
under the porch
emerge too early
scavenge for pollen
in the final days
of winter
find nothing
to sustain them
look for another
porch to build
a new nest

The Wounded Warrior of East Boston Terrace
Cyndy Muscatel
Fiction

Sara had a scar under her chin, right at the end where it met the jaw. She'd forgotten about it, but then her granddaughter cracked her chin open. All the blood reminded her of when she was five and jumped off a wall. Like Humpty Dumpty, she'd cracked open — but just her chin.

Isn't it amazing, she thought, how childhood memories remain so intact? She could see the action of The Chin Drama roll in her mind as if it was streaming from Amazon Prime. It happened right after the family moved to their new house. Before, they'd lived in an apartment, and Sara had played all day long with Chi Chi and Linda.

But there were no girls in the new neighborhood — except for the two older Hansen girls up the street. One summer afternoon when her mother sent her upstairs to rest, the girls appeared on the porch outside her room. Sara had been listening to *Helen Trent* and hadn't heard them until they tapped on my window.

"Let us in," they said in unison.

She glanced at her door, then rolled off the bed.

"How did you get up here?" Sara whispered through the small space of window she opened. Her bedroom was on the second floor. Outside was a large deck — a Dutch door opened out to it.

"There's a ladder against the side of the house," Gretchen, who was ten, said. She scratched at the window screen like a cat after a fly.

"Open up your door. We'll come inside and play," Katrina said.

Sara stepped back from the window. The girls seemed like evil wizards, repelling and enticing her at the same time.

"Come on, come on," they whispered in unison. "Open up, open up."

She didn't want to let them in — it would be going behind her mother's back. Besides, her room would never feel safe again if they roamed through it. Before Sara could make a move, they heard Mother calling her name. The girls scurried from the window, across the deck to the ladder. They clambered over the side of the house and were gone.

One afternoon later that summer, the girls knocked on the door to see if Sara could play. Sara didn't want to go, but her mother shooed her out the door. They lived on East Boston Terrace, a street that was a circle. Although it was in the heart of Seattle, there were lots of woods around. And a haunted house. It had slid from its foundation and lay in ruins down a ravine. Rumor had it that a baby had been killed and was buried under the huge blocks of broken cement.

The girls started up the street, walking by the Peterson brothers, who were shooting rats with bows and arrows. The biggest brother held one up. Skewered on an arrow, blood ran down its fat body. When it opened its eyes and stared at Sara, she screamed and ran across the street. The other children couldn't stop laughing.

Further up the block was Mr. Nichol's house. (He always gave them a nickel on Halloween.) The Hansen girls ran to his driveway and started climbing the retaining wall.

"You're not supposed to go on other people's property," Sara called out.

"Don't be such a baby," Gretchen said.

Nimble, she was already at the top, walking its narrow space as if it were a tightrope. Katrina was right behind her.

So, what was Sara to do? She knew it wasn't right,

but she started to climb the wall. Not as strong as they were, Sara struggled to pull herself up.

As soon as she stood next to her, Gretchen put a hand to her forehead.

"I can't take it anymore," she wailed. "Goodbye, cruel world!" With that, she jumped off the wall.

"Goodbye, cruel world," Katrina, in her turn, yelled. And jumped.

Now Sara was alone at the top of the ledge. She looked down to where they stood. It seemed very far away. But, like a lemming, she cried, "Goodbye, cruel world," and jumped.

Her landing wasn't as elegant as theirs, but she thought it was safe. It felt like she'd scraped her chin on the rough cement, nothing more. The Hansen girls' screams and pointing fingers told her otherwise. When Sara put her fingers to her chin, they came away bloody.

Gretchen ran to get Sara's mother while Katrina walked her toward her house. Blood cascaded down her front.

"Maybe you should hold onto your chin," Katrina suggested.

She did, but blood ran through her fingers.

Halfway home Sara saw her mother running toward them, Katrina at her side.

"Sara, what have you done?" her mother screamed when she saw her.

"I scraped my chin when I jumped off Mr. Nichol's wall," Sara said.

"Yeah, Mrs. Mann, we were just playing, and Sara followed us up," Katrina said.

Sara's mother cut her off. "She's only five. What were you girls thinking?"

She grabbed Sara's shoulder and started pushing her towards home. "How could you do this to me?" she hissed.

Tears welled in Sara's eyes. Her chin hurt, and her mother was so mad.

When they passed the Petersons, the boys stared at Sara. *They probably think I'm more of a scaredy cat than ever*, she thought. But then the oldest Peterson boy stood tall and saluted her. His two brothers did the same.

Sara straightened her shoulders and lifted her chin. She walked proudly past them, the wounded warrior of East Boston Terrace.

How Can We Bear It?
Claire Scott
Poetry

We talk about bearing grief, five stages
to see us through so we don't break
every window or swig bottles of red wine
books and books and books written
to guide us through grief's bleak corridors
of furled promises and failed prayers
until we reach Acceptance
entire shelves at Barnes & Noble
Bearing the Unbearable, Finding Meaning in Missing
hundreds of grief counselors waiting
to take your money and soothe
your grief in only forty sessions

We talk about bearing pain
ninety-eight results for *Pain Medicine Near Me*
scads of yoga and meditation classes
breath your way to a better life
do twenty-seven sun salutations
sit in silence an hour each day
pain doctors hawking on every corner
holding signs, shoving each other aside
ready to relieve the pain in your ankle, your knee,
your neck as well as headaches and hangnails
and don't forget the miracles of pharmacology
like Fentanyl, Vicodin and Oxycontin

But what of tenderness
with its soft eyes and thistled tongue
no one teaches us how to bear its touch
how to dare when wide wings have atrophied
and caged hearts flutter song-less
how to dare when you feel the flash of a fist

the forever of fear in a locked-in closet
how to let the rusted hands of a clock click
and turn, how to swallow cool night air
or watch a rose unfold its delicate petals
how to dare let go and allow yourself to fall,
wings sprouting, settling into the arms
of someone waiting, someone wanting
to receive your wavering heart

Pomegranate Seeds
Claire Scott
Poetry

If I defer the grief I will diminish the gift
—Eavan Boland

I tried to protect my daughter so if
her pet guppy Pearl died (again), I
bought another Pearl to defer
the pain, the tears, the truth, the
loss of innocence, the great grief
of mortality ringing her bones. I
buy an identical one so I will
not notice the death, to diminish
my sorrow, to distract her from the
seeds and rob her of the gift

How Did This Happen
Claire Scott
Poetry

We believed — how could we — if we got them to
twenty-one we would be *ollie ollie in-come-free* no
worries about coming home at two am or flunking
geometry these offspring of ours with fresh degrees full
of hope and hype in nothing worthwhile — what were
we thinking — so back home lugging dirty laundry & a
hunger for home cooking can't hang a *no vacancy* sign
after all these are our children with dreams we don't dare
deflate despite the restive needle at our hand — trying to
be the most mother we no longer want to be—a tentative
launch living with others circle back to the bedroom
with airplanes Snoopy sheets & grimy plates with dried
catsup under the bed — time-lapsed learning or
excessive coddling — what I want is a simple supper
with a glass of cabernet what I want is not to listen to
cockeyed plans for a start up in cauliflower jewelry what
I want is not to worry about resumes & job interviews &
starched shirts & bus schedules but what I really want is
my turn.

the lake folk dead
w v sutra

poetry

the lake folk dead lie in the scotty boneyard
glidden street being all filled up or almost
there also lie the townies and the river folk
but the sea folk dead are different fish for sure

its mostly sacks of ash these days you know
economy being needful to the last
it gives the living one less thing to fret about
on the gentle ridge with all its ordered stones

the native folk have left their oyster middens
their feasting lodges now are earth again
they named the river for its little fishes
as pemaquid our tranquil lake is known

grandpa raised our swampy lot with fill
when a tree got in the way he cut it down
our mom put fresh pond lilies on the table
you go to jail for lilies nowadays

we kids were sent into the lake each day
to pull the eel grass wading to and fro
and all along the cove new camps were building
at the end of every dock a brand new boat

we stacked the grass in heaps upon the beach
and the dads went out on weekends with their guns
they killed the snapping turtles without mercy
so little kids could keep their little toes

they got some big ones posing with their trophies
but you know they never did destroy them all

and now the warden roams the sacred waters
his only care to bring the scofflaw woe

so put me in that boneyard when I go
my body well and truly pulverized
arising from a past no one remembers
a mockery made of all my heaped up goods

on the ridge
w v sutra
poetry

if you stay we might could fix
that run of fence where the deer
slide through like ghosts
leaving fur on the barbels

and those places where
the trees come down
bending the pickets and stretching the wire
with all the work to do again

how will i lay a straight line
without you at the other end
shifting your weight like a nervous horse
when i approach awkwardly

i wonder if you really know
the fate to which you led me
if you stay i may tell you
when the moment arises

see how this stretch of pasture
has been bitten down
how greedy horses are
how thin is all this soil

and the trees
i wish we had more poplars
in our grove instead of
these black walnuts

the walnuts break and fall
lightning kills them

for all that they feed
the wild pigs

as for you and me
let us stay and become this farm
the horses stamp the frozen ground
let the earth swallow us here

the good scout
w v sutra
poetry

jupiter and saturn in the southern sky
son and father each the other
now mute glowworms
late gas giants
courted by the stars
in their silent perspectives

on my back on the hard ground
of a barren mountain field
listening to my father
as we lay encamped
as he named the astral bodies
in their myriads

earlier that day he sent me to the village
to buy bread in a language not my own
he supplied me with a word in the arabic
khubz that the baker understood
and i returned with enough for ten
thus we make men of our sons

now comes the goddess with her golden lamp
now comes the reckoning of merit
much have i heard about illusions
much have i learned about deception
long will i remember the good scout
who named the morning stars to me

Pruning
Scarlett Peterson
Nonfiction

On any given day, a massacre of tomato leaves. These pruned shoots a sign of my procrastination, of writing I should be doing.

Nearby, a ruckus of wings — one face of the flytrap swings on its stem, a common housefly hanging half out of its jaws.

I glance between my dogs and the back of a neighbor's house. The sound of a child's frenzied cries reverberates off of the vinyl siding, crescendo against the voice of a screaming parent. Voices punctuated occasionally by the sound of violence.

It's September, late for tomatoes. Mine press on, bear a third set of blooms.

The fly struggles to free itself. A voyeur, I catch it on camera, trim the footage down to a few seconds of beating wings.

My neighbors leave the windows open while beating their child.

Some tomato leaves tell you when to prune them, curl, turn yellow, develop holes edged in brown veining.

The fly frees itself while I'm not looking, hovers above my notebooks as if to tell me of its success, to brag its own strength. To taunt me.

All is quiet soon, no more sounds of hands meeting flesh.

I toss overripe fruits at the fence, land them in the far corner of the yard. A dead spot of clay, now home to a pseudo-compost pile. I hope the flesh of the fruits richens the soil, readies it for future growth.

The spotted dog gnaws on a stick she's unearthed from the tomato detritus.

New growth on the tomato plant is purple against the yellow blooms, the old green growth.

Formerly raised voices have gone silent. The house radiates, exhaustion and spent energy coming off the roof in waves.

The dogs scratch the door, begging for comfort, a fresh bowl of water.

Fish Out of Water
Edward Michael Supranowicz
Art

Forgotten Things 1ac
Edward Michael Supranowicz
Art

Trapped Between Night and Day
Edward Michael Supranowicz
Art

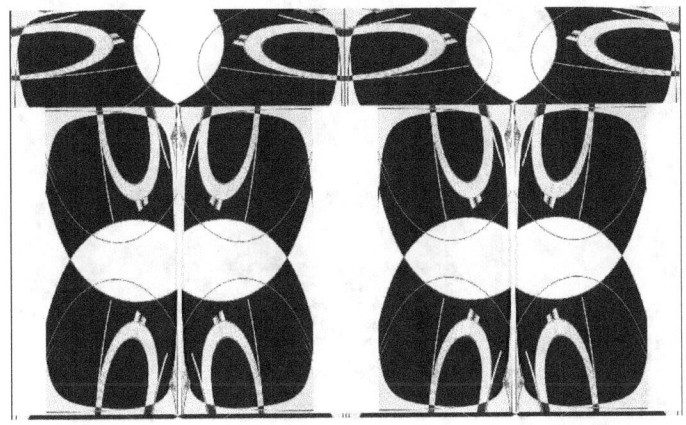

Facing Away From the Horizon 4
Edward Michael Supranowicz
Art

The Hornes at Midnight
John Grey
Poetry

The wind is Arctic.
The time is midnight.
The moon's a crescent.
Trees are black,
snow on them likewise.
The ground is smothered
in a foot of winter.
All is sparse.
Even the faces.
Even the universe.
A question was asked
an hour ago.
No one wants to be
the first to answer.

Life's a mall.
Life's a busy city street.
Life is neon.
Not a farmhouse.
Not a silent family
in a tiny den,
unthawed by hearth
or bare bulb
shining down.
Only life can say,
"I agree"
or "I disagree."
And then there's
the rest of us.

Famous Writer's House
John Grey
Poetry

On another tour of a famous writer's house,
I stand behind a rope
and take in details of her parlor,
bedroom and even the bath
where she soaked
and perhaps thought up her ideas.

The kitchen table is set
with plastic food.
But the shelves are lined
with the books of real people.
And there's a desk
in her drawing room
where she wrote her words long hand.
Just looking at it
gives me twinges of
carpal tunnel syndrome.

I've spent time with Twain and Hemingway,
even stood outside a Hart Crane abode
though I didn't go in.
I even stayed at the Charles Dickens hotel.
Of course, he didn't.

But, more than just
indulging in their words on paper,
I'm a sucker for where they lived,
sat down to eat, read the newspaper,
quarreled with their wives or husbands,
spat and chewed and bathed.

It makes them seem ordinary
which in turn
makes their accomplishments
even more extraordinary.

I plant my feet
in a famous writer's footprints.
But, sadly,
the next step is all mine.

Walnut Greens
Mary Grace van der Kroef
Poetry

Heavy with green
spheres.

Weighted
to bend low.

Shake a branch,
release,
gather,

baskets brimming full.
Blessed by heaviness in
buckets.

Time
to shell the walnuts.

Falling Purpose
Mary Grace van der Kroef
Poetry

Rustling like paper
Something not quite right

Curling edges
Unlucky sail
Or maybe ...

A rolling tail
Travelling over pavement sealed

Scrapes of character
Notches of wisdom

It wares,
Disintegrating,
As journey works its sandpaper sadness

Remains
Threads, the ghosts of waving life
Rest in gutters
Adding to the soupy slush

Fallen leafage finds it's end ...

Or newness?
Drain sips these memories of trees

Taking essence
Down rivers to quenches nature's thirst
For life

Right to Breathe
Corrinne Brumby
Nonfiction

Florida longleaf pines creak like floorboards as they sway in the breeze; their needles rustle, roaring like ocean waves.

*

We create wind when we exhale in a mini rush. Yet when it's not a shout or an intense sigh, we take breaths for granted. We forget they are there, so commonplace that we don't notice their value, how much we need to breathe, that simple motion of air pumped in and out of our lungs.

*

Pines are breathing CO_2, exchanging it for the oxygen we need. I've heard it said that trees are our lungs. And in a lesser sense, we are the lungs of the trees, a symbiotic relationship of breathing. We are all breathing.

*

In the beginning, the earth was brought to life by breath. The divine breathed and there we were and there the trees were and grass and animals and birds.

In Hebrew, the word for spirit is רוח Ruach, which means breath or wind. Spirit is the life force of a living being, that deep core that transcends body, and in that ancient language, it is literally breath.

Everything that has breath, therefore, has spirit.

*

"I can't breathe," were a man's last words, as someone took that right to have breath, from him. His plea became the cry of a people outraged by suffocating racial injustice.

One of my biggest fears is drowning, holding my breath as long as I can, then gasping for air, lungs filling with water. The other scariest way to die: being strangled or choked, not able to take in a new breath, no more right to breathe.

יֵשׁוּעַ Yeshua of Nazareth died from not being able to breathe. Every breath on a cross is excruciating effort, until you are too weak, too in pain to pull yourself up for another breath.

Loon and other animals dove deep into the water, but they could not hold their breath long enough to reach the soil on the bottom. Then muskrat dove deep into the seas that covered the earth, holding his breath as his lungs burned for air. He reached the soil and nestled it in his little paws. As he swam to the top, his lungs were emptied, filled with water; the light faded as he floated. Nanabozo took the soil that muskrat gave his last breaths for, and with it formed Turtle Island.

*

Yoga centers around breath. Breath brings balance to the mind, body, and spirit. Focus on the deep inhale, air filling your lungs until they are full of life-giving energy, and a long slow exhale, releasing all the tension, all the stress, all the pain pent up in your body.

We often forget to breathe.

I breathe deep, calmed by the weight of my body on the floor, bowing to the earth in a child's pose.

*

Sugarcane will burn soon in the everglades as it does for harvest every year. Wealthy white communities require burns to be postponed if the wind is blowing towards their communities, avoiding the effects of smoke. U.S. Sugar doesn't care if ash rains and smoke chokes the poor black communities of the Glades, burning cane freely as smoke suffocates black children in school. Apparently, white people have also claimed the right to breathe.

The west is on fire. All smoke and no air. My friends have headaches and can't breathe.

A virus of the lungs has survived over a year, infecting millions worldwide, no longer able to breathe. My great uncle Bob, infected with the virus, breathed his last.

*

How long can we live without air?

Long needles rustle like waves as wind blows.

We count the seconds the world has held its breath.

I am a Daisy
Corrinne Brumby
Nonfiction

Bare feet patter on grass still holding the morning cool
as the summer sun bakes my skin. The soil gives under
my steps. The willow's draping branches, like an elder
woman's uncut hair, brush my shoulders. For a moment,
I enter another world, a sanctuary for children and
fairies.

I step into the blazing sun. Train tracks and buzzing
powerlines stand beyond but I tune them out as I walk
among the wilds between two ponds, reminiscent of
ancient Illinois prairie. I pluck cattails that look like
hotdogs and imagine eating them. I plunge my finger
through the brown peel and pull out white pillow fluff.

Scattered amongst the cattails are the auras of fairies
and gods. I smile because they smile. Daisies are sun and
clouds tethered to the ground. I pluck one and hold it
close, inhaling the gift, smelling earth and heaven at
once.

I carry the daisy home, gazing at it between steps.
My mom shows me how to press it: place two sheets of
paper in the pages of an encyclopedia, trim the stem and
lay the flower flat, close the book, put it back on the
shelf, and leave it.

I fill more books with daisies.

*

At 18, I leave home and go 500 miles away to find the
God I forgot was in the daisies. At ministry school,
hundreds of hungry believers gather to find God in a
building. I don't miss home. I believe I have found
where I belong, believe that my family is missing it, that
they aren't spiritual enough.

I spend hours in manmade walls, trying to find the divine, while disconnected from the divinity I knew as a child, disconnected from my flesh and blood, from my ancestors.

I find a daisy growing in a patch of meadow and pick it, caressing it in my hand. I admire it the whole way home. I nestle it between two paper towels in my journal held tightly shut with an elastic band.

*

I visit home every few months. I feel different, out of place. I mourn my childhood gone. I mourn the distance from my family. I start to miss home.

I visit in June when wild daisies are blooming in remnant prairie. I meet with my maternal grandparents, Baba and Papa, for my late 21st birthday. We reserve a table on the 91st floor of the second tallest tower in Chicago. Panoramic views overlook the city. Cars, people, and buildings, even tall ones, are miniatures. The Ferris wheel spins atop the pier. Tiny sailboats glimmer in the sun on the vast lake.

I am Freya in the clouds.

I walk with Baba and Papa to a table beside the windows. A square vase holds a bouquet of giant white daisies with a Happy 21st Birthday note stuck inside. I can't turn my gaze from them as I sit like a queen in my black and daisy dress.

Baba says daisies were Great Grandma's favorite flower. I return to my childhood, to my roots. I remember Great Grandma and I watching Mr. Roger's when I was five. She would call my mom to see if I could stay for dinner. She made the most delicious Polish food and had pet canaries because she loved how they sang. I can see her smile and her snow-white hair, and hear her voice as if she were still here. Through the daisies, I feel connected to her, and wonder why I ever left.

*

Daisies find me wherever I go, radiant sunbeams that grow where land has been disturbed, blooming where you wouldn't expect beauty to grow, in ditches, in construction sites, in the yard, fighting through all the mowing.

My ancestors call me back home, back to my roots, back to myself whenever I wander, whenever I seek something I forgot I already have. They whisper in my dreams: *Corrinne. Corrinne... Maiden, Innocent, Pure, Beautiful. Remember who you are.*

*

I gently remove the elastic band from my journal. Nestled in between memories and paper towels are pressed daisies, still preserved after years. I consider using them, gluing them to a card, or some other decoration. Instead, I close them in my journal, safe in my memories to forever remind me: I am a Daisy.

Valentine's Day
Joel Harris
Poetry

Outside my window —
the warmth of two rock pigeons
nibbling each other

Dear Scruffy Pigeon
Joel Harris
Poetry

It's about time that I properly introduce
myself. I am the young lad you snoop on through the
bedroom window at the edge of the PVC
eavestrough, sitting stately in my executive
chair, clawing my way through *Metamorphoses*, or
some quirky, paramodern gibberish trying

to pass itself for *avant-garde*, cyberpunk cool.
I do notice you like to drop by outside, but
I really don't appreciate your droppings, the
bile runniness of it, the way it grimes; how it
reminds me of seasoned callaloo infested
with tiny, squirmy maggots mothered in the cave

of your dwindling, claustrophobic bottom-hole.
Still, you amuse me, the way you contort your neck
in the manner of a circus performer, the
way you instrumentalize your tough beak to scratch
your lilac hackle, your tender breast and other
teeny, private parts frustratingly hard to reach.

The way you strike that *Vrikshasana* pose with one
tibia lifted in the air, standing there on
the hot galvanize sheet, about to engage the
contemplative life; the *bindi* of your third eye.
Our landlord has tried everything in the book
to rid these colonial premises of your

kind, but like a lowly Beetham squatter citing
your damn rights, you stubbornly return to roost like
a case of bad flu. You most certainly enjoy
the heady view from up there: the broad shoulders of

the windy Maraval Valley; the garland of
forest growth sticking out like rough, ingrown hair. I

just wish you'd scratch a tad less for both our sakes.
It's considered bad manners in human circles.
Don't you know it's terribly rude to scratch yourself
in public? How's your youngling coming along these
days? I pray he's fine and dandy. Anyways, I
wanted to say howdie, to welcome you home mate.

love poem that hangs from a cliffside
Nora Smith
Poetry

…

cherishes the breeze // even as the grip loosens
and the jumping animal // in my chest readies to
meet the rocky coast // that is rushing up now

…

have i not looked at you
gazed past you into that
present moment? have i
not gripped your hand
tighter like you might stop
pulling the sun down
inch by inch? have i not
relinquished all control to
your primal instinct which
left me abandoned for
hours, true, but jilted to
sit quietly in the dunes
and on the rugged cliff
and knowing that while
you trekked back to me
that i was also an
imprint in the snow
of your sweet feelings
which pile up high over
the hours and afford me
such a soft place to land

…

we were not lovebirds and i am relieved
that for you i did not cajole, or warble
instead — and look and feel my bones
where they hum through my creature
body — i am writing this between

moments of bliss, moments that hang
from your lips, then a cliff, and then?

i know i have falling left to do
crash and see my skeleton
                              stick through

I Destroy Jewelry
Allyn Bernkopf
Poetry

You, who engraved me
into thin necklace, sloppy
infinity loop titled "Un-
stoppable Love" & how
I hummed over its metal,
like I found a compass

to you, thought you finally
loved me with a gift of white
gold. You told me it was diamond
& I told you it was priceless
You etched the nickname you
gave me, "Textbook," into

its white spine. "Textbook"
because I was "safe." Because
I didn't jaywalk. Because I
didn't speed, didn't text &
drive. Because I followed

recipes, followed rules, read
all instructions. "Textbook"
because I read, because I
wear gloves to pluck roses,
because I wire the chicken
coop more shut when you

said it was "fine" (a racoon
sure appreciated that) & do you
remember the fight we got in
when I'd do it anyway? Wear
gloves, twine more chicken-

wire, crossed at crosswalks

& how anger simmered
in the car when you'd text
behind the wheel which led
to volumes and volumes
of arguments lacerating
our house walls? So yes,

I took a kitchen torch &
melted the necklace down.

On Finding Out I Might Be Infertile
Allyn Bernkopf
Poetry

I pack up my house
place trinkets in boxes
sealed with a kiss of tape.

Poetry books line my walls
while the child statue reading
is nestled in thick socks to keep

her warm. Safe from damage.
She's next to the statue
of a teacher, a grown woman

wrapped in gloves. She holds
her books tight to her chest.
I stuff extra socks, blankets,

and bras around them. Carefully
close cardboard flaps above fragile
heads & move on to the next box.

Your Card
Tony Abbott
Poetry

It was an hour of purple shadows,
the afternoon on early winter days
when seagull ghosts loop violet over the sand.

The old year is choking out, confused and shriveled,
while the future brings nothing yet
to set upon a table broad as the horizon.

When your card came,
mentioning death at a care home, it was one more
memory to settle in the box before sealing its lid —

with just enough now, an hour maybe,
to make the sign of the cross, bid our ghosts
fly off over the sand, and lift our eyes to the sea.

Beckoning with a Sigh
Bill Wolak
Art

The Whisper's Mirror
Bill Wolak
Art

Moon Walk
Alexandra Williams
Poetry

I walk at night
where the Ridgeway guides my feet: a silver thread
throwing the darkness around it
into chaos. Barley rasps at my ankles
and the moon is a night light
and you, *everywhere and nowhere*

if you were real
Linda M. Crate
Poetry

sometimes i think you were just someone
i conjured into being, a vision that i needed
to see before i lost a part of me that i couldn't
afford to lose;

i remember the freckles that dotted your face
and your radiant smile more glorious than the
light of a thousand suns strung together —

i remember your soft skin brown like the spring
after the first rain before muddy season where the
world whispers a need for her flowers and ever
so glorious in it's beauty against the dullness of my
dark and dreary day,

you said that you couldn't get your selfies to quite
turn out right and i couldn't help but say out loud:
"but you are cute" and i don't know if you heard me;

yet there are still days full of wonder of you and if i
simply conjured you up in a dream or if you were real.

Crushed
Charles K. Carter
Poetry

You plucked a cigarette from my pack
and placed it between your plump lips,
using your own lighter to ignite.
We were standing on your balcony,
without pants, mid-coitus.
We needed a break from the heat.
The chill in the fall air
raised the hairs on my thighs.
You leaned on the rail,
looking out into the sky
like you had found the answer
to one of life's many mysteries.
I looked across the street
at the vacant playground equipment
of a vacant pre-school –
empty swings, forgotten joy.
For a moment, our conversation
was as raw and naked as we were.
We talked about trauma
and about anxiety medications.
But then you rattled on about video games
before crushing your cigarette butt
in the vintage orange glass ashtray
before taking me by the hand,
leading me back inside
to finish what we had started.

Just Wait
Kevin A. Risner
Poetry

for the kickback from motorcycles to shoot out and
jar the street from sleep
as if anyone could sleep
most nights now

we wonder whether another person is lying
on the ground with life leaking out
simply sit in a pool, a light blue plastic version
of childhood, flip-flopped feet soaking everything in

car air freshener around neck
an umbrella drink in hand
Bruce bellows how he's *Born in the U.S.A.*
as a tinted view of the world transforms

into unforgivable lies
everyone sips on Polaroid pasts
looks at the TV
searches everywhere for what they want

to be told, what they want
lives around them or inside them
or inside a humming screen
inside a humming season

believe it all
every single syllable
the first taste of summer
even the second is not truly fresh anymore

when windows open wide
when the air comes back in

when the world takes
the deepest of breaths

and waits
for everything
to calm down
we'll be waiting forever

The Atlas of Your Back
Phil Goldstein
Poetry

Rediscovering the soft grip of your body, like waking
up to snow, bright & miraculous as it clung to our hair,
soft
flakes raining in the gray morning light, sheep bleating.
Such delight in the familiar yet ecstatic.

For years I've been fog — formless, rolling
in off the Sound, silently away from you.
I forgot how touch can be electric, the sweet taste
of your lower lip, how to kiss, even.

It was like I was a boy again, before I had ever seen
a woman naked. I was only familiar
with my own sex, in hidden moments
in empty rooms, pulled onto cracked basement floors.

You helped me remember so much,
like what it means to be lost inside a world
where all I can feel is your back, all I can smell
is your hair dangling softly on my forehead.

On the Stairs
Rashmi Agrawal
Fiction

Sejal kicked at the channel gate of the old lift. It was stuck again, sixth floor this time. In the last one month, she had to climb the stairs seven times after waiting for long.

She huffed on the third-floor landing. A door flung open behind her. Catching her breath, she straightened herself and sensed someone standing close by. Taking account of her surroundings, she turned.

It was a man holding a magazine. The cover was half-visible; a semi-nude woman, probably an actress, was sucking on a cherry. He flicked its pages, but his eyes skimmed through Sejal, up and down.

She skittered up the stairs. *Just one more floor.* He licked his pinkie as long as Sejal could see him from the corner of her eyes.

When Sejal complained about the elevator, Mom said, climbing stairs would tone her legs. Sejal was tired of swallowing this same excuse. She fiddled with her thumbs against each other and decided not to talk about the weird man.

The next time when she climbed the stairs, the same man was puffing away a cigarette. When Sejal crossed him and asked to make way for her, he blew out ringlets of smoke. As soon as those curls hit her face, Sejal ran. Two steps at a time, smokey ribbons still hanging midair.

The lift was under repair the next day too. Its door was jammed on the first floor. Sejal desperately waited for a company to climb the steps with. And before long, a lady appeared with groceries.

Sejal grabbed that septuagenarian's basket out of respect. The lady smiled. Before Sejal could engage in small talks, the old lady bid her goodbye and entered a flat on the second floor. The girl panicked. She closed her eyes, prayed to God, and took quick strides along the railing.

The man, clean shaved today, stood in a fresh pair of jeans and a vest too tight for his size. His perfume, though strong, couldn't curb his body odor. His lips curled as if about to whistle.

Sejal ran towards her floor.

When Sejal complained to her mother about this mysterious man, Mom rolled her eyes. You don't need to stop there, Mom said. Just keep climbing if the lift doesn't work. And we'll complain about him if he troubles you again.

As if on a cue, the elevator didn't break down or get stuck for several days. No one blocked it on the higher floors either — fifth, sixth, or seventh. But its machinery was rusty and tattered; it had to malfunction. And when it did, Sejal found the man holding a glass on the stairs right outside his door. A strong smell hit her. *Whiskey?*

What's your name, baby? the man asked, swirling his glass. You'll enter high school next year, eh?

Sejal's lunch roiled in her stomach, seeing him grinning. She was standing at the center of the landing. He was sitting in front of her. When she didn't answer and tried to avoid the stalker while crossing him, the man stood up with a jolt, brushing his skin against hers. She faltered but managed not to trip. Sejal's backpack fell with a thud. Her bottle leaked, and water spilled. She coughed loudly and ran upward. She didn't turn back, didn't throw side glances, and crashed into her mother as soon as the door opened.

An hour later, Mom took Sejal to the third floor and pressed the doorbell of the suspect's flat. Sejal picked her bag and the sipper.

When Sejal explained, the beautiful lady with auburn hair and red lipstick at the door blinked a few times. No one with this appearance lives here, the lady said, and slammed the door. The other flat had a big padlock.

After a week, Sejal had to take the stairs again. The lift first kept her waiting for over ten minutes. It was stuck on the seventh floor. When it appeared on the ground floor, it got crowded before she could enter. So, she took the staircase.

Sejal rang the bell of the septuagenarian on the second floor she had helped. The lady greeted her with a smile. After listening about the man, the lady suggested staying alert and carrying a repellent bottle, or skipping all occasions to climb alone. *But how?* It took a minute for Sejal to realize the old lady meant *pepper* spray.

Not a bad idea, Sejal thought and decided to buy one that night.

As she reached the third-floor landing, her eyes scanned the vicinity — the green climbers and pink flowers; the gerbera and succulents; the cheerful painting on the wall and the terracotta items in red, blue, orange, and other bright colors.

She mustered courage and rang the bell of the other flat, which wasn't locked this time. The owner denied having seen that prowler. He looked at her with raised eyebrows and at her bag and black shoes and the white-green school uniform. Sejal cleared her throat and left. She was worried about how could someone stalk her so close to her home, so close yet far to be visible to anyone yet.

Days later, when Sejal took the stairs again, hand clutching the spray, a clamor vibrated the stuffy air. Murmurs of people hit her like a fly's hum. Irritating and unceasing.

She gulped as she reached *that* floor. Cops were going in and out of *that* house. The lady's auburn hair was messy and lips chapped, her kohl smeared. Someone has murdered her husband and planted evidence against her, a neighbor murmured. Of course, such a lovely woman can't kill her husband, another neighbor whispered.

Sejal rose on her toes on the staircase from where she could see the dead man. *That* man.

The lady with auburn hair winked at Sejal. She had lied earlier. And the stalker was now removed from the stairs. Sejal hugged her mother. No more abandoning her precious minutes, waiting for the lift.

End

Bad Apples
Karen Boissonneault-Gauthier
Art

Evening Comes Down
R.T. Castleberry
Poetry

As we wait for a death
these things are visited upon us:
Train whistle's warning
cascading a travel grievance.
The bird that charmed at daybreak
disappears at Evensong.
Reordering the nature of ruin,
ninth month moonlight grips
failing edges of icing pond,
mud-furrowed harvest field.
Sundays are spent sleeping
under a fan, beside the phone,
scuffed floor piled with
tossed clothes, church programs.
I've not taken a steady step this week.

A Spacing of Days
R.T. Castleberry
Poetry

I square my debt in landlord limbo,
shake a final Evensong psalm
from this creaking balcony,
these bird's nest eaves.
A pointillist screen of rain-dripping trees,
green-dark splashes of paint, mud, moss
demonstrate no loss.
Chimney's chipping smoke reeks a last stew.
Ending checks are cut, readied for *Cash*.
This house, a grievance, seized me once.
I've served it enough.

A Parish of Famines
R.T. Castleberry
Poetry

Mockingbird says it's
no day for crosstie walking,
no weather for Jim Beam and boo.
Preparing for the Second Coming.
I'll need wings and waffles,
a switchblade sidekick
to carry me to that throne.
Pocket watch out for pawn,
I pull creaking cowboy boots,
a pearl snap wedding shirt and
take myself down to Maceo's.

Death's head walking stick cuts
along the sidewalk grid,
margins of phone line, skyline, tree line.
Hinge creak of wind-rocked door
cracks the silence, skims off
patched streets, oil slick puddles.
Small fires flaring in the stores,
streetlight white blazes smashed glass.
Not a calming spirit,
I wonder how many
dreaming days before I lose.

Across Dauphine Street,
starving dogs sneak and bite,
armband rangers shuffle in lines
under a showcase marquee.
Tipping a forty-dollar hat
I take the last outside table,
greet the evening prelates
with indictment rumors,

the clash of insinuations.
I ask the waiter,
"Has Elijah come with the mail?
Bring me the usual with
a pack of Chesterfields.
I'll see the supper menu now."

Afterglow
Matthew Schultz
Poetry

It is easy to forget
the light and I are Gemini,
twinned and bound
to the encroaching dark.

Symmetrical aliens
of inexplicable chance,
Our obligatory dimming
seems to go on forever.

And So It Goes
Robert Pegel
Poetry

Find a way or make a way.
Life is malleable, bend it
in the direction you choose.
Refuse to be a victim
of circumstance.
There are limits in time
which confound the mind
and overcome the spirit,
if we are hardened by experience
and not softened by love.
Truth sought after awakens
the soul to no longer play
a game of chance,
with a life looking for
our utmost devotion
to detail during days
lasting longer than our energy
can withstand.
Witness and be still.
Survive and continue
to a place where dreams
never die.

Just Sleep
Robert Pegel
Poetry

Can't wait to fall asleep.
Maybe we'll meet up
in a dream that I will
remember in the morning
and you will come back
to life in all your splendor.
Hearts won't be broken
and life will continue
the way it was supposed
to be.
The future won't be derailed
and the wind will always be
with our sail.
Love's journey will last
as long as it should
and see us through.
Sleep will be the catalyst
that captures moments
awake in the subconscious
where the relaxed mind
melds with wishful intention
where everything is perfect
for a little while.

Hibernate
Robert Pegel
Poetry

I didn't choose this life.
This life chose me.
Was willing to be somewhere else.
If it was heaven,
I don't remember.
Now I'm here.
Found out this life is overrated.
Still, I've got to make the best of it.
They say you only live once.
What if I've already lived
and died in several lifetimes?
I choose to sit this one out.
Will you let me rest
for just a little while?
Cause I'm bleeding on the inside.
And I've got memories of a morning
that will haunt me forever
etched in my mind.
Sorrow and regret,
steal the sunshine out of most days
and rob the moon
of its light.
My heart is broken.
My brain is exhausted.
My eyes can barely open.
I need to sit this one out.
Wish I could lay down and hibernate.
I promise I'll get back in line.
Return to this lifetime.
You know I won't be a problem.
I'll keep up with the group the next time.

May Thy Slumber Be Blessed
Sharon Goldberg
Nonfiction

For my great nephew Aaron Eli

You were born during a pandemic. You were born before your parents were vaccinated against it. You were conceived before a Covid-19 vaccine even existed. Your Mom, my niece, calls you a miracle baby, not just because of the pandemic, but because she had four miscarriages before the egg that became you implanted successfully in her uterus and grew and grew and grew.

What could be more hopeful than a new life?

I met you when you were five months old. Three generations of our close family gathered to celebrate my 71st birthday, my 70th celebration having been postponed a year because of the pandemic. Ten adults and six children including you, the youngest, reunited at a house in Breckenridge, Colorado, during a lull when the pandemic subsided and before it resurged as a new variant.

We bonded, I think, you and me. You smiled at my guppy imitation. You stopped crying when I sang *She loves you yeah, yeah, yeah. She loves you yeah, yeah, yeah*. I sang the same song to your oldest cousin, Marco, when he was a baby; you can't go wrong with the Beatles. You'll learn about them later, perhaps from Marco's Dad, your Uncle Jeremy, who appreciates music from the 1960s, a long, long time ago. When I see you again next year, pandemic permitting, I'll sing "Brahms Lullaby." Your cousin Jordan asked me to sing it over and over at bedtime. *Lay thee down now and rest, may thy slumber be blessed*. It's my favorite lullaby, the one my Mom, your Great Grandmother sang to me when I was a child. I felt safe and loved when she sang it.

Like so many families in the 21st century, our clan is scattered across the country. Distance presents challenges in the best of times, but since the pandemic began, we've felt the sting of separation and ache for connection even more. It will become part of your story that you were born in Denver, unlike your brother Jonah who was born in New York City. Your parents fled Brooklyn when Covid cases surged there. They sheltered with your Aunt Rebecca, your Uncle David, and two cousins and, after a year, decided to stay in Denver. They bought a big house just a mile from your aunt and uncle. They chose family. They chose fresh air.

Your Mom will make sure you get all your childhood immunizations. And when a Covid vaccine is ready for toddlers, you'll get that, too. I remember how hard she worked to earn a PhD in Public Health, even traveling to Nigeria to research childhood immunizations. Our family believes in science.

You were born during a time when people wear masks for protection, a requirement in many situations for those two years old and older. Since you often see people in masks, do you think of them like hats or gloves or pajamas or any other item of clothing? Or do you find masks disturbing because they block facial features and expression? I hope when you're two, no one will need to wear a mask. I hope when you start school, all classes will be in person and masks will be a thing of the past. I hope when you trick-or-treat on Halloween and wear a ninja costume or Harry Potter costume, masks will only be used for disguise.

When you're much older, you'll learn that more than 800,000 people in the U.S. and more than 5.4 million in the world died from Covid. Those numbers frighten me. I wish I could wear a funny face or brave face for you always, but my anxiety is a chronic bass line to the melodies I sing. Scientists say Covid probably won't go away. Even if we reach herd immunity, which means further disease spread is unlikely, or the virus becomes endemic, which means less transmission, fewer hospitalization and deaths, we'll still need booster shots periodically as we do for the flu. And Covid won't be the last pandemic. I wish I could guarantee you'll be untouched by the next one. I wish I could promise you'll be safe from all dangers like climate change, gun violence, the erosion of our democracy. I wish I could assure you that when the next pandemic emerges, we'll be more attuned to science and less compromised by politics. We'll have learned from our mistakes. We'll act faster. We'll act better. We'll contain the pandemic earlier. I wish. I hope.

Perhaps, precious Aaron, you'll study plagues and pandemics in school. Maybe you'll take after your Mom who will tell you about the months she spent in Nigeria and what she learned about social norms and immunizations. But for now, you're free to explore the world from your stroller. Free to play and play with fluffy and shiny and dangly stuff. You're oblivious to pandemics and other problems. Just like all little kids deserve to be. Happy. Safe. Protected. Loved.

You will always be loved.

Menudo Poem
Vincent Antonio Rendoni
Poetry

The first time I have menudo
is at the restaurant where Abuela
doesn't have to pay.

We're far from alone.
The men who work with their hands—
men in orange vests and salt-stained flannel—
stare into their private pools of hominy and fat.

Even though we are
a people apart, here we are one,
breathing and salivating over
liquid communion,
noting how close we are
to the Lord and how much
it smells like fresh oregano.

May you know the distinct pleasure
of filling your stomach
with another.

May it give you that ancestral
feather-serpent energy
for the bad days
that will come and go.

May it turn your fist into a blade
and give you the power to cut down
anyone who dares to fuck around
and find out.

The Door in the Back of Your Neck
Vincent Antonio Rendoni
Poetry

Abuelo picks at a scab and says
beware of the door
in the back of your neck.

Let no hands touch it.
It's where thoughts come from.
It's where thoughts go.
Let no hands touch it—
especially your own.

Today, he *me enseñará* a lesson.
Going to work that curandero magic.
Going to loosen up that belt
and do a little dance.
Coughs up a block of stardust
and tamarind into his hands.
Pounds it into some pepperleaf—
from up his sleeve—
and rolls it into something fat.

A puff, a pass.
A wheeze, a laugh.
A tap at the door
in the back of my neck.

Then, I'm neither here nor there.
There's stars and darkness,
a horseshoe pit, warm beds,
yellowjackets bringing meat
back to their nest.

The crackle of butter.
Smells of cinnamon and avocado honey.
Sopaipillas in the kitchen, someone
cooking me something sweet.

A lawn covered in salvage and scrap,
mint creeping, penetrating the rust.
A tire fire, warming me, choking me.
All those engines that'll never wake up.

Crows in heat—they're coming for me.
I can see them for miles, and still
it all feels so final,
so abrupt.

Abuelo's big red hand
grabs me by the scruff.
Pulls me back topside.
Slams the door shut.

His lesson complete:
See what is never
too early
to see.

Tamarind Soda

Vincent Antonio Rendoni

Poetry

My sister and I meet for lunch when we can.

We always go to the same old spot: a taqueria
built into the burnt-out husk of a Taco Bell.

Nature abhors a vacuum.
Wants to fill it with manteca and corridos.

Reclamation.
Who are we to fight such a beautiful thing?

Been coming here since we were kids.
My sister doesn't remember.
She's not much for remember when.
Now she has kids.

She makes me wonder what we look for in old places.

El Gordo y La Flaca plays on mute.
In the corner, someone's put out crystal and silver.
There's a healer with purple hair, moving from table to
table.
She chants. She hams.
She opens her fist and reminds us:
this shit isn't free.

My sister gets the carnitas—
She knows what she's about.
I get the buche—
Gotta prove something to myself.

And though her eyes only ever look forward,
something flickers when I order a bottle of tamarind
soda.

We split it down the middle in Styrofoam cups.
Our secret handshake
no one can take away,
no matter how white we become,
even when she smiles and says
she never really cared for the stuff.

Tell me, she asks,
Do we actually like this
or only because Dad did?
with a laugh.

It takes us home.
Just close enough to know
we're so far from it.

Better This Time
Gail Denham
Poetry

Is there a time when whatever
has to happen, happens. Perhaps
it's come by one other time
and we were too busy to notice.

This time we pay attention. We're
older now, wiser (one would hope).
We watch it, study it closer,
sort of like a favorite TV re-run,
one we never quite remember.

The characters and conditions aren't
always the same. At least the incidents
stir old thoughts, lost memories. We
enjoy things more this time. Our
purpose now is to make the best of it.

We sit very still. We notice
everything, refuse stress.
Seems better this time.

Send Me The Pillow
Gail Denham
Poetry

"Send me the pillow that you dream on ..." Today,
the post office would charge a lot to ship this feather-
filled pillow — a pillow possibly older than the singer.

In those days, we didn't throw away anything. Jar
lids became ash trays; soda bottles turned into clothes
sprinklers; empty medicine containers held small
bouquets; rags were dust cloths or saved for a quilt.

We had one heavy iron skillet, a Dutch oven for Mom's
marvelous Sunday roasts, sauce pans she received when
she married, and threadbare blankets. Pillows were kept.

If I desired current fad clothing, such as a cashmere
sweater or a clear wind breaker that friends wrote on
at school, it was 50c a week paid from my hourly wage
of 75c an hour at the Dairy Queen.

We never suffered hunger or felt deprived.
I rode a hand-me-down, one speed boy's bike
everywhere. Few cars sped through our quiet streets.
Long soft ball games at the vacant lot caused me
to let potatoes burn, dinner Mom asked me to start.

A quiet time. Dime a song on the juke box
at the drugstore soda fountain; now every time I hear
that song, I still taste 10c cherry cokes.

Boots' First Adventure
James Bone
Fiction

Boots had no interest in what *they* called 'self-improvement'. Her Mother told her she should see a doctor. She didn't think she was sick. She didn't feel sick. She felt OK. She lay in bed all day on her left side, staring at the wall. She read online about Japanese teenagers that end up staying in their rooms for the rest of their lives. She liked that. She thought it sounded OK. Her brother said she was 'Othering' them. She had no idea what that meant. She looked it up. She felt bad, so she wrote them a letter. Her Mother showed the letter to her doctor. He gave her a new pill to take every day with breakfast. It tasted odd and made her use the toilet often.

Sometimes, they'd lift her up, her Mother and her brother, and they'd try and force her out of the house. She wouldn't resist, just lie motionless as they screamed and cried and pleaded and whispered and threatened. They tried starving her; for three weeks she was given only water and occasional slices of bread. This made her ribcage look strange in the mirror. She liked the way it looked. She told her Mother this and her Mother threw her mug of hot tea across the room. It spilled all over her computer and notebooks. The next day she was given a big plate of spaghetti and she threw it up all over her bedsheets. Ghosts visited her every night; she'd talk to them about everything. They were friendly ghosts, not haunting anyone, just there to lend a sympathetic ear. You speak to them too, sometimes, probably, when you think you're alone.

They tried to bribe her. "Come with us! Come with us to the shops, we'll get a nice new computer!" She knew they could easily buy her a new one online. There was no need to leave the house nowadays. The people out *there* could do it all for you. Boots felt nothing when her brother snarled in her face, about how lazy she was, about how ungrateful she was, about how she was making her Mother ill. Her Mother seemed OK to her. She didn't see any reason why anyone should feel ill.

One day, on her twentieth birthday, her Mother brought in her favorite meal, six eggs scrambled with butter and salt and pepper, and sang her 'Happy Birthday' and said your brother has hung himself with a rope. She said she cut him down and tried to save him, but he had broken his neck and the ambulance and police came and took her statement and took his body away. The funeral was on Saturday. Today was Tuesday. "Will you come? Please?" Boots shook her head and lay down on her left side, staring at the wall. A little bit of egg dribbled down her chin and fell onto her pillow, and she wondered if her brother would be a friendly ghost, if he would listen rather than haunt.

Tangled
Shannon Barbour
Nonfiction

At thirteen, I raged against my hair. I'd stand in front of
the mirror, my hands wrapped in and around clumps of
curls, and tug. Tug in the hopes it would straighten. It
was an angry vanity.

At a Homecoming party in seventh grade, I sat on a
dull beige sofa talking to a boy. The boy matched the
sofa, but it didn't stop a friend from falling for him. She
fell headfirst and whole bodied. The next Monday,
whispers surrounded me. Walking to the buses after the
final bell, a different friend accosted me, accused me
with her question: "Why did you kiss him?"

The main telephone in my house hung slightly above
eye level on a small wall at the back of the kitchen. The
cord puddled on the floor. My parents must have bought
the cord separate from the phone, it's spiraling length
disconnecting conversations from stationariness.

I clasped a tattered-edged picture I'd ripped from
Seventeen. I showed my hair stylist the waifish model
with unevenly cropped hair certain she would not agree
to so drastic a cut. But she did. She left longer strands
that curled around my earlobes. She gave me layers. She
gave me bangs. She gave me a cut meant for straight
hair. "Helmet Head" is what my sister said.

At thirteen, I sported braces and glasses and ugly,
unmanageable hair. "Kiss who?" I asked. All that day, a
rumor swelled that I had kissed the dull boy on the dull
sofa. Despite his abject refutation {"kiss *her*?"} and my
denial, the rumored kiss cemented itself as a truth.

Listening to my friend, the one who coveted the dull
boy, cry and berate me from her end of the telephone, I
pulled at the coiled cord. I tugged and stretched until a
flattened, straightened section lay against my hand. I let

go and it recoiled. Interrupting her with an occasional
rebuttal, I otherwise left the line open for her anger,
which spiraled and spiraled. I curled into the cord,
wrapped it around my waist and spun a slow circle until
I was tangled.

The quick *beep beep* of call waiting gave me
opportunity to shirk my friend's endless whining. On the
other line, a different friend in search of the truth. I said
I'd call back. *Beep beep.* "Hello?" Another friend
jumped on the attack: "I can't believe you!" I said I'd
call back. *Beep beep.* "Hello?" This time it was the dull
boy, "I guess we should talk?" I said I'd call back,
though I doubted I would. When I clicked back to the
line with my injured friend and her fuming, broken
heart, she met my "Still there?" with a tone of renewed
injustice: "Who could be more important than me right
now?" *Beep beep.* I ignored it. Her presumptive anger
continued. *Beep beep.* I ignored it.

My curls have haunted me. I have flat iron burns and
the invisible scars of nicknames: Helmet Head and
Bozo. Even as an adult, I've had an unsteady
relationship with my hair.

Beep beep. I ignored it. I'd lost count of the minutes
it had been since I spoke. *Beep beep.* I couldn't listen to
her anymore: "I have to take this."

I expected exasperation or indignation. I was
prepared to continue with my defense, my refutation of
the rumor. I was not prepared for the breathlessly
panicked voice of my grandmother. "Hello? Shannon
where is your mother? I've been calling and calling." I
stammered an answer but she talked over me, her words
running together. "Where is your mother? He's having a
heartattackIthinkheisdying!"

The phone still cradled between my cheek and ear, I
pressed my finger onto the switch to hang up. Instead of

a dial tone, I heard my irate friend: "Who was *that*? Was it him?"

My grandparents had a telephone in the kitchen, too. Theirs sat on a squat table in the breakfast nook. The cord wasn't long, like ours, so there was no walking and talking, no space even to sit. They had a second phone in the TV room on the other side of the house and one in their bedroom at the top of the stairs. My grandfather's heart gave out out of reach of any phone. Which phone did my grandmother run to? She'd been *calling and calling* she said. Did she sprint back to him in between all the times I didn't answer?

A favorite thing for my grandmother to say was that she wished she had half my hair. Her own hair was thin and then sparse, and I don't remember a time when it wasn't gray and cut short. She slept in pink rollers hoping curls would imprint. Sometime in her mid-eighties, she asked me to help her decide on a wig. It was an endearing vanity.

I kept the phone pressed to my ear. I'd held the phone for so long, physically hanging up seemed an impossibility. Relinquishing the phone would precipitate an unalterable future.

My hair falls out. I'm not losing it; my hair isn't thinning but regenerating with a speed and profuseness that has become a source of amusement. My daughter laughs at the stray hairs left on sofa cushions and counter tops, the ones that cling to shirts and bedsheets. I often want to collect those curls. I want to somehow stitch them together and send them through time to where my grandmother still playfully tugs at my hair, saying, "oh, if only."

I swipe at my phone's screen, my thumb reaches for the phone icon. Numbers appear, but there is no dial tone. It's the noise I am after, the hollow echo of an empty line. I listen anyway. Listen to nothing.

Lonely
KJ Hannah Greenberg
Art

Matineé
Steven Anthony George
Poetry

like animals in the forest
I've mewled for sweets
to touch to my lips
like animals in the forest
plucking and scratching
we were speaking French
we were animals and speaking French
as the sun filtered its golds
through the canopy
and I like
a faun
danced on a stump of oak
you pulled me down onto the litter of leaves
and like the animals we whispered
each to the other in whining tones
and the scent of burnt twigs
from the distance flowed over us
like animals in the forest
you kissed me deep
and I heard the night to fear
come crawling and you
like animals in the forest
had something from inside me
in your hand and I droned like
a badger in a trap
as you laughed

Your Perfume
Meghan Kemp-Gee
Poetry

I think sometimes that I would like to leave
everything to the last minute. I think
I'd like to slice up my life and feed you
the very last slice. To the last minute,
I'll leave everything. At the last minute,
I'll have every last thing I almost
didn't have. I'll have you trailing off, a
final swallowed syllable of smoke, of
stopping where the grass becomes the trees, of
not stopping, of becoming, of the trees
swallowed up by wildfire, then becoming
wildfire, like the world become wildfire, like
red and white, red-white, white, sickly red and
soil-white, of tracking what is fleeing
through those firetrees smelling of that last
relentlessness, of the last minute where
I've left you where I'll see you running bright
and headlong through the smoke.

While my Mother Worked Saturdays
Kalyn Livernois
Poetry

Do you remember me, cropped bangs
and the cavity between my front teeth
like cracked pepper? I can still picture
your hair   white-blonde   and the way
you squinted into the sun when we were
halfway down the eastern slope. We'd stop
for lunch, always the same American cheese
singles wrapped in cellophane and lidded
cups of Nesquik — strength to finish the climb.
The mountain, so huge beneath our tiny
bodies. I will always remember it this way —
never as the hill beside your mother's house.
Everything always transformed by the place
my frame is fixed   in the territory

Ode to My Poetry Professor
Gina Stratos
Poetry

don't make it rhyme
automatic failure
rhyming is for dead
white men, and I
am not deceased

hip hop is not poetry
beat breaks aren't line

breaks

and line breaks are *fundamental*

but let the words hit'em
unlike *glorious*
which means nothing

anything, everything

write   v
           e
           r
           t
           i
           c
           a
           l
           l
           y

let the absence of whiskers
in a sink be the divorce,

the hooded wolf,
your clitoris

unpack your issues
with the church, with God,
so, I cancelled therapy
and bought more books

How to Deal with a Fly at a Buddhist Retreat Center
Fran Zell
Nonfiction

Always check for flies before opening the door to your living quarters at the Buddhist Retreat Center. Ants may be climbing up the door or hanging around the stoop. Brush them away quickly before opening the door, but don't let ants distract you from checking for flies.

If a fly gets into your living quarters it may be because you were too focused on ants, and flies are by far the more troubling. They buzz around and dive bomb into food. They are annoying. Silence is the promise of a Buddhist retreat center, and flies don't know from silence. True, there are other creatures at the center that go about their vocal business: a hummingbird moth, for instance, rising from tall grass with its throaty signature roar; the white horse whinnying in the pasture, head held high as it carefully skirts the electric fence; the grass itself blowing in the wind, a fly buzzing through it.

It is one thing to listen to a fly buzzing through the vegetation outside your door, another thing entirely when the fly invades your living space. It's like the difference between your ex haranguing you in your memory mind, and him actually right there, standing in front of the kitchen sink bellowing because there is no more coffee in the house.

You must be very careful about what you let in upon opening the door because you must not kill another living creature at a Buddhist retreat center. Death is a natural part of the life cycle and leads to rebirth, says the Buddha. But, nonetheless, you do not want to be the instrument of death.

The fly gets inside anyway. It is in the bathroom, buzzing around when you brush your teeth. You ignore the fly and the fly lies low. But the fly reappears that afternoon when you return from a bicycle ride. It buzzes around the big garden salad that you have placed on the table near the open window that offers a view of bluffs and valleys and trees in the full green regalia of August. It is an exquisite view and you do not want it spoiled by the fly.

Bam! You shut the window, trapping the fly between the glass and the screen. It buzzes up and down the screen, looking for an exit. It is trapped in there, and you suppose it is suffering. But suffering is part of life, according to the Buddha. The Buddha believed that most suffering is caused by desire, and that the way to end suffering is to eliminate desire.

You are suffering watching the fly suffer. You don't want to let it suffer so much that it dies. You might as well have rolled up the *New Yorker* magazine you brought with you all the way from Chicago and swatted it dead right away. But you didn't bring the magazine with you to become an instrument of death.

You finish eating, wash the dishes and decide to open the window, releasing the fly from its suffering. The fly dashes out of its trap and wings across the room, buzzing around your head, as if to say "thank you." Or maybe it's saying, "ha, ha, you were suffering more than I. My desire to drive you crazy was greater than your desire to get rid of me."

But you let that thought rest, because the fly is now buzzing low to the ground near the door. You open the door and it darts back outside. Quickly, you shut the door, congratulating yourself on how well you have learned how to deal with a fly at the Buddhist retreat center.

Soon you go outside to sit in the sun and read, to enjoy the hummingbird moth whirling through the grass, the white horse wheezing in the pasture, crows cawing from far across the valley, the steady low hum of crickets, the sound of gravel softly crunching as a man walks silently down the path toward another Buddhist retreat center cabin. Occasionally there is the muted sound of a passing car on the state highway in the valley, a quarter mile away.

You go back inside to spend the rest of the afternoon meditating. There is a fly in your living quarters. For a moment, you wonder if it's the same fly. But it doesn't matter. It's a fly. It's there against your desires, distracting you and causing you to suffer.

Suffering is inevitable, says the Buddha...yada, yada, yada...

The fly buzzes past the chair where you are sitting and onto the window pane. You open the window. The fly enters the space between glass and screen. You close the window, trapping the fly. This starts a whole new cycle of suffering for you and the fly.

Time is endless at the Buddhist Retreat Center. Sooner or later the fly will either die or you will relent and open the window again to release it.

To relieve your suffering, you go out for a walk into the valley, past the horse chestnuts and into the remains of an old apple orchard, its twisted and gnarled trees weighted down with unharvested fruit. You go to forget your suffering and the fly's suffering, hoping that the fly will not be dead when you return. Just to make sure the fly will not be dead, you open the window before you go, releasing it into the room.

You grab your cell phone, take a forbidden glance at the news you have been trying to avoid all day: Hurricane Ida upgraded to a Four, about to make landfall in Louisiana where hospital ICUs are full of Covid patients. Another explosion in Kabul.

Aha. The fly is more than a distraction. The fly is your need to remember that suffering follows you everywhere. Now that you have realized this, there is no more need for the fly.

When you return from the walk it is gone.

Looking Back
Corey Mesler
Poetry

Though I did most of the work
I thought we'd built
something together.

Now the walls are broken
and sunlight stabs through
the holes in the drywall.

Weeds choke the kitchen like
old food. In the attic a
pair of mice once lived.

I found their bones, light and
white as thistledown, on
this first day of winter, looking back.

Didn't it take forever
Corey Mesler
Poetry

Didn't it take forever to
get here? Didn't you
change your mind a
thousand times? Wasn't
it wild, and frightening?
Wasn't it strange? Love
the strange. Didn't you
wonder who was beside
you? Didn't you blame
everyone and yourself?
Wasn't the lie a terrible
temptation? Wasn't the
stranger the worst part?
You're not alone now.
You're not the only one
afraid. Love the part where
you don't trust yourself
completely. Wasn't it all
a mystery play?
Love the mystery at play.
Love the strangeness in you.

The simile
Corey Mesler
Poetry

The simile slipped
in
quietly,
holding its shoes,
because
it knew it was
late
and it did not want
to wake
the reluctant reader.

ARIES
S.T. Brant
Poetry

Prize-fighting war gods don't butcher men
With the frequency or the righteous spine
The way animals are butchered. When
        Artists
        Rage
        Inadequately
        Everybody
        Suffers.
Forests catch fire with disgust
From our horrible diplomacy with Nature.
Can the World control the world; or Chaos, chaos?
No more than medians can guarantee obedience
Against the powers of the sheep they shepherd.
        So what's to do?
        Accept no effort less than All;
        Recognize no futility;
        Invoke your powers,
        Edit out your wrongs;
        Stay strong.

LEO
S.T. Brant
Poetry

Fading in on
    Life,
    Eager
    Only children
Find for themselves their own kingdoms;
In other families, siblings
Apostate their bloodlines
To gain a larger portion of the poverty
They're due. Securing every entrance,
Every exit; rusting every mechanism
Used to operate the draw bridge,
And neutralizing any potential strike, aerial,
Doesn't fortify royalty from regicide, as the world,
    Lionhearted,
    Engages
    Offensively
Against mortal challengers to its natural reign.
A more skilled swordsman, as Nature is,
Will eventually exploit the wielder only of a shield.
Fading out,
Looking at the world, I see
Swords are shields,
Moats and catapults:
Mere antiques in museums;
The cavalcade of fiction in my mind,
Parading through me,
Is dissected among the different branches of my veins:
But everything always repairs at my heart,
From where my soul
    Looks
    Eagerly
    Out.

graveyards
Mark Belair
Poetry

the shortcut to saint francis grammar school / wove
through the church's graveyard / a route my sister and i
took / depending upon the weather

we balked at dark-cloud days / that threatened rain / and
left home early / to walk the well-traveled / small town /
sidewalk way

but in fair weather we ventured through / either ignoring
the gravestones / or pausing to parse
a near-vanished name / note a freshly fallen stone / a
crumbling crucifix / a pot of dried-out flowers /
memorials for the dead / themselves decomposing

after our family moved to the suburbs / my sister and i
went to separate schools / mine a public / and i took a
yellow school bus that would stop for kids attended by
parents / then trundle off / the driver in frowning charge /
the landscape speeding by outside / including

a distant graveyard / the sight of which always haunted
me / without frightening me / something i couldn't
explain / until it disturbed / one morning / a memory of
our old graveyard walk / a memory dug up like a
disinterred body / a memory of once having felt / so
close to life

The Smell of the Car Wash in the Morning
Mark Belair
Poetry

Broke
is why you work at a car wash,
out on the sidewalk,
rag in hand, drying fenders
still dirty from the dysfunctional
machinery inside.

Broke
is why you put up with the humiliation
of showing up each morning
ahead of time
to stand in a row
the owner will pick the dayworkers from.

That others were
broke worse than you—they were poor,
while you were just college tuition-stretched—
was why, after a few weeks, you couldn't bear
to be chosen, then even stopped going:
someone's kids—your fellow supplicants,
all recent immigrants, were all family men—
suffered as a result.

You can still picture the owner
stepping out of his chauffeured Cadillac
he had washed somewhere else
and, before taking his pick
of immigrants, drawing
a deep, dollar-filled, All American
smell-of-the-car-wash-in-the-morning breath.

Dankness
Mark Belair
Poetry

The old, gritty sidewalk
holds hard

evidence of a soft
spring shower,

a loamy aroma
that rises

up from cracks
that reach

down
to the fresh, muddy

time
before

men
with concrete

purposes
arrived.

Signature Required
Sarah Ferris
Poetry

She holds the divorce Judgement
and cold slinks in, slithers
along floor, scents
a warm ankle, curls up calf
                behind knee
curls 'round thigh, buttock
to the waist and enters
like an epidural, spreads
along hips, over tummy
up ribcage, back of arms
down past elbow to hands
                fingers
cold,   cold   fingers
and movement is difficult,
movement becomes
painful and so it's time.
Time to move, time
to sign and be released.

Leashing a Teen
Sarah Ferris
Poetry

I worry about my teen starting to drive,
wanting to go off by herself as she
pulls hard at the leash, yes

we're holding on
as she pulls the choke collar tight
and it's taking both of us

just to stay the path
as she sniffs the undergrowth —
because we know, oh yes, we know

the meat in there that attracts her and
where we buried our favorite bones.
Yes, we have to hold on

hold on, double up the leash,
hoping it's strong enough
hoping we're strong enough

and you know, it would be nice to have
a pair of elbow-length padded gloves,
the kind they use to train attack dogs —

cause sometimes   the teen turns on us
like a bitch in heat, and   snarls with
narrowed eyes   but we remember, oh yes,

we remember and reach out slowly to her
like those who calmed us so long ago
when we snapped the leash

so we hold on tight, sometimes
taking turns sometimes together,
as we slowly give her full reign.

An Owl's Call at Dusk and Dawn
Sarah Ferris
Poetry

A hum fills the silence
between short, deep
owl calls. The hum that's

my constant companion,
tinnitus. I don't think about it
anymore — I weave it into

ecstatic union with
sounds around me
and make it song —

otherwise it'll drive
me crazy. Because
there are no crickets here

there is only tinnitus,
so I weave that
constant high note

with the owl's short,
deep ones and as self
glimpses self, I stretch

beyond loss of hearing
into that small death where
I can hear my own song.

Calorie Counter
Corey Miller
Fiction

I'm an overachiever, surpassing the Freshman 15 by gaining 50 pounds. I employ the online calculator to decipher how many calories I should eat daily to trim fat. I enter my height, age, and current weight to discover 1,689 will transform me skinny, where eyes won't divert onto my core. I increase the age 100 years and the calories required for survival drops to 1,246.

I add another 100 years = 942.

Another.

At age 381 I won't need to eat anymore — I may simply exist.

I will hide until then. Complete my Child Development degree online behind a filtered avatar of how I wish to appear.

I planned on raising America's next generation, but it's easier to give advice than swallow your own medicine. I could teach How To Seem Content Living Under The Radar 101.

Online claims a calorie is a unit of energy defined by the amount of heat required to raise the temperature of water by 1 degree. My body is 60% water. My body is 98.6F. How cool will I be when I'm 381? Ground temp? Enough weight to snowflake from a cloud? How hoary must I become to calculate self-worth? Fingers crossed my student loans are paid off by then.

I eat 7 grains of basmati, belly ballooning with shame. I'm a treasure map beneath this fat, how a twig might costume an inflatable sumo wrestler for Halloween. Growing up I believed it was "Hollow Wean" as if weaning off food that doesn't melt in your mouth, direct deposit of sugar to the blood stream. I deepthroat a pickle to release everything inside me;

vomiting a self-help book, memories of my boot camp
father pinching my rolls, skipping prom because no
matter what I goddamn do — the scale tilts upwards.
Merely a midnight snack.

On my dorm desk rests a 85 calorie fun size
Butterfinger and *Health Magazine*, displaying
reproduction stimulation of model ribs jetting out,
underling "Top 10 Ways To Maintain Your Beach Bod
Through Winter." Just because something lies before
me, doesn't mean I need to consume it, I tell myself.

I flip through my $125 *Child Development* textbook.
The 297 pages are thin like running through a deli slicer.
The pages morph from the flat broad side into a narrow
line you hardly notice, yet enough of them bonded
together can create an entity of value.

Hunted
Phil Huffy
Poetry

Look about the cabin,
quiet in its resolve
to reveal little
of the mayhem seen.

The plank door lies unhinged
near the huntsman's remains.
A single gas lamp
renders him grotesquely.

Nothing has been taken.
His skiff bobs in its slip
as the pond awaits,
but the wait will be long.

And he does not listen
as the steel covered roof
amplifies raindrops
from branches overhead,

propelled by ghostly gusts,
inclined in their falling
to dancing rhythms
briefly, brightly beating.

The killer trots away
blithely, on massive paws,
having satisfied
his curiosity

though finding the huntsman
a pitiful trophy,

easily taken
but unappetizing.

Pick A Word
Madinah Jolaade Abdulsemiu
Poetry

Pick a word
Write your thoughts
Let your pen heal your world
Through the veil of courage

Be the weaver of your thoughts
Never write with a borrowed word
For the world comes around for it
And you will be left sinking underneath.

Set your mind ablaze with words
Set the world on fire with thoughts
Then the mightiest soldier will bow
And the shiniest king will bless
For winning hearts without bloodshed.
But with inks of wisdom and drops of knowledge.
To follow and be followed,
In lines of words and stanzas of thoughts.
And not tears of lost ones.

Change the world with your pen
And not with your sword.
Write till the ink in it cries
Let your pen be a deity
And be the mastermind behind it.

Image 2
Madinah Jolaade Abdulsemiu
Art

Calamity Jane
Olivia Ivings
Poetry

Florida's summer opens when a plague
of cicadas ascends in March.
The luckier states are still enjoying spring.

I want to bubble up like an Icelandic geyser
and razor myself skinless, as I tell my boss
when she asks how I feel.

A second-grader asked why I have a mullet.
I want to join a women's punk group, but I play
banjo. I'll learn more during my Saturn return.

My bare feet dangle off the porch swing;
Mars is a glowing speck from my view.
I met a woman in the bar's bathroom last week.

Tonight, she's tattooing, "Even Sad Cowboys
Say Yeehaw" above my kneecaps. Life's candor
and the way mangroves buffer the current wreck me.

Past Deaths
Beatriz Seelaender
Poetry

I never again want to be part of anything
any movement, sudden or complete with a manifesto
when you're part of things they are part of you
and the other parts will twist and pull at your insides
you try to take it apart, it's resistant
it's a shooting pain that goes dormant hopefully
after some five years. Until something happens
and it feels exactly like someone has travelled
back in time precisely to kill you
fifteen-year-old you, discounting her blessings,
back on her bullshit after one day trying to be hopeful
or nine years, who knows? if I told her
the pain takes this long to get over, she'd
do something drastic like drop out of high school
and we can't have her doing that, we depend on her
to pull through to exist. but somebody shot her tonight,
and I am still here. This she would not have survived,
yet somehow I did. Rules of time travel are to me
abundantly clear. So how come I'm all right,
my shadow self notwithstanding? My novel
shooting scar
that I just got, from the past pending?
A jammed printer finally passing me a note
in it there are expired aspirations and bad news
I somehow missed the first time around, I didn't know
So that's why I made it, then, I missed the memo
So embarrassing for a girl to be emo in her twenties
But then you have to stop making sculptures out of ashes
and calling each of them a phoenix

feel like dying
Beatriz Seelaender
Poetry

sometimes dying your hair makes everything better /
sometimes drowning your roots in neon blue makes you
feel put together / like some instafamous cool chick /
some manic pixie girl of your dreams / an infamous
2011 hipster who drinks alternative water / a full person
without her original trappings / free from character traits
and their tethers / free to be anyone who might be happy
/ and responsible enough not to let the roots show / your
folks say you're so lucky to have this hair / they don't
know that what makes it lucky / is precisely that it can
be / squandered and depleted in artificial dye / that
makes me feel like a real person / a phenotype squared /
paint it blue / paint it black / bleach it so maybe it will
reach my brain / feed my strange hunger for wasted
things / so that it won't devour the rest / call me emo all
you want / but when I listen in repeat / to welcome to the
black parade / I listen to the version in jazz

QWERTY Girl
Joe Gianotti
Poetry

She hung art on her walls,
filled composition notebooks
with musings of love and time.
A music goddess,
who collected Lorde and Lana
when they still played the Vic.
Stand-up quipster.
Sketch wisecracker.
Improv farceur.

Normal will not alter your course.
Chanel suits everyday of the week?
It's difficult to find images
of Plath in anything informal
or Kruger in a smock.
Lizzy only leaves Upstate in couture.

The weapons of war
will always outpace strategy.
Her path just a shade to the left
of the one envisioned.
She'll learn that talent
born to blue-collar work ethic
has only two possible destinies:
personal fulfillment
accompanied by familial disappointment
or a life of misery
paired with parental praise.

She will learn to reach out,
to touch the forest's trees,
to swim in the 2 a.m. lake,

nothing between her skin
and the clear water beneath her chin.
She will shout truths to the sky,
and whisper secrets to the ground,
and at the end of the day,
she will alchemize
her blood into language
that does for the class of 2040
what Alaska did for her.

Apocalyptic Haiku
Mark Jackley
Poetry

Way after Basho

moon melted,
pitch black,
barnburner of a war

Listen
Mark Jackley
Poetry

I dreamt my words streamed up my legs. Reverse tears.
After all these years, I shouldn't be surprised.
True language comes from somewhere deep, the pools
below speech. Dark, wet places. Where things drip.
From under stones too, like the ones around my mailbox,
baking like potatoes as we glide around the sun,
warm and rough and real in my wrinkled hands, a note
from when I was a boy and the table opened wide.

RAW WAR
Jay Mora-Shihadeh
Poetry

raw war
bled for
no reason
on curdled
tongues.

taste, sour
slice, blood
moon, red
sun, black
dawn, never.

night forever
forgot to shed
the days bitter
dark cold.

silver guns
on young
skin,
hobbled knees,

dreams wet
humidity.

sour taste
left on right
raw war
powerless
endless
thoughtless,

no mercy
left,
or right.

the poet, at 45, looking at a blank piece of paper
J.C. Mari
Poetry

Don't keep
Yourself from me, like
Women allowing themselves
Only at a distance
Passage birds in gaudy sight
The story of other men's lips
Other men's hands,
Don't

Make yourself unavailable
Like the voice of God
Thundering only for the insane,
Murderous or elect,

Don't become
A thing of yesterday
Like clotted blood in a corpse

Don't go
The way color goes
From childhood photographs:

Don't keep
Yourself from me
Like the life that's
Flown off into some other distance ...

Contributor Bios

Tony Abbott
After starting writing poetry, I detoured for the last thirty
years or so to write novels for younger readers and have
now returned to poetry for adults. I am interested
primarily in epic verse, and two of these poems belong
to longer sequences, but may stand up on their own.

Madinah Jolaade Abdulsemiu
Madinah Jolaade Abdulsemiu is a student of Mass
communication at National Open University of Nigeria,
Kano. The Ekiti writer started showing up her talents at
the young age of 8.

Rashmi Agrawal
Rashmi Agrawal has been published in nearly a dozen
anthologies. She lives in India and sits by a big window
to write and enjoys diverse seasons outside it while
scratching her brain (and whatever comes in the way) to
polish her first novel. When she's not writing, she vexes
her daughter in motherly ways. She tweets
@thrivingwordss.

Shannon Barbour
Shannon lives in central Mississippi with her husband,
daughter, and four dogs. She especially loves writing on
rainy days when her favorite candle is apropos of
everything, a scent called Thunder Storm. Or maybe it's
just been raining for so long.

Mark Belair
I'm a poet/drummer and, amazingly, there are many of
us. Perhaps, either way, we simply let rhythm be our
guide.

Allyn Bernkopf
Allyn Bernkopf is a Ph.D. poetry student in the vast plains of Oklahoma where she binge-watches the Marvel universe, drinks too much wine, and antagonizes her cats all to procrastinate what she should be doing; homework. She's a millennial, so she has GAD, PTSD, and ADHD, and she'll tell you all about it but, as the joke goes, does the bare minimum to fix it. She enjoys little things like coffee, poetry, and waking up at the ass-crack of dawn.

Robert Beveridge
Robert Beveridge (he/him) makes noise (xterminal.bandcamp.com) and writes poetry in Akron, OH. Recent/upcoming appearances in Feral, Ez.P.Zine, and Homology Lit, among others.

Karen Boissonneault-Gauthier
Karen Boissonneault-Gauthier is an Indigenous artist/photographer creating cover images for Synkroniciti, Pine Cone Review, Feeel Magazine, Dyst, Arachne Press, Wild Musette, Gigantic Sequins, The Unmooring, Vine Leaves Literary Journal, Gateway Review, Doubleback Review, and many more. Walking her Siberian Husky named Kiowa under an aurora borealis is forever a dream. Visit www.kcbgphoto.com for all her endeavors.

James Bone
James Bone is a twenty-six-year-old writer from Liverpool, England. His interests include pigeons, silent cinema, rap music and walking. He enjoys writing semi-autobiographical work concerning mental illness, drug addiction, trauma and chocolate.

Timothy Boudreau
Timothy Boudreau's recent work appears in Trampset,
Reckon Review and MonkeyBicycle, and has been
nominated for Best Microfiction and a Pushcart Prize.
His collection Saturday Night and other Short Stories is
available through Hobblebush Books. Find him on
Twitter at @tcboudreau or at timothyboudreau.com.

S. T. Brant
S. T. Brant is a teacher from Las Vegas. Pubs in/coming
from Honest Ulsterman, EcoTheo, Timber, Door is a Jar,
Santa Clara Review, Rain Taxi, New South, Green
Mountains Review, Another Chicago Magazine,
Ekstasis, 8 Poems, a few others. You can find him on
Twitter @terriblebinth or Instagram @shanelemagne.

Corrinne Brumby
Corrinne Brumby is a neurodivergent writer who lives in
Orlando, Florida. She lives in Florida and loves getting
outdoors and connecting with nature through hiking,
birdwatching, kayaking, and simply being outside with
the trees and birds. She writes to inspire people to
connect with nature and find the courage to be
themselves. When not outside or writing, she loves
hanging out with family, traveling, eating good food,
and playing the violin.

Charles K. Carter
Charles K. Carter is a queer poet and educator from
Iowa. He holds an MFA from Lindenwood University.
His poems have appeared in several literary journals. He
is the author of Chasing Sunshine (Lazy Adventurer
Publishing), Splinters (Kelsay Books), Safety-Pinned
Hearts (Alien Buddha Press), and Salem Revisited
(WordTech Editions).

R.T. Castleberry
R.T. Castleberry, a Pushcart Prize nominee, has work in
Steam Ticket, Vita Brevis, San Pedro River Review,
Trajectory, Silk Road, StepAway, and Sylvia.
Internationally, he's had poetry published in Canada,
Wales, Ireland, Scotland, France, New Zealand,
Portugal, the Philippines and Antarctica. His poetry has
appeared in the anthologies: Travois-An Anthology of
Texas Poetry, TimeSlice, Anthem: A Tribute to Leonard
Cohen, and Level Land: Poetry For and About the I35
Corridor. He lives and writes in Houston, Texas.

Linda M. Crate
Linda M. Crate has been called weird since she was a
child, but learned to embrace her weird and what made
her different because it made her happy. She has always
loved stories, music, and art for they made more sense to
her than any "logical" math problem she was given. Her
favorite season is autumn for it feels like a second spring
with an explosion of color that nature pours her heart
and soul into.

Gail Denham
As a poet, I chose the smallest item to write about, trying
to have fun with the subject, dragging up and
highlighting old memories. My goal is to make people
laugh or remember. My muses are humor, faith, fun,
crazy when I can.

Sarah Ferris
Sarah Ferris grew up in a library masquerading as a
home with innumerable older sisters who dropped books
on the floor, so the baby nibbled paper and devoured
type until her green eyes turned brown. She writes about
the everyday, reveals familiar things in a new light, and

devours books wherever she roams. She lives in Los
Angeles with her family.

Sharon Goldberg
Sharon Goldberg is a Seattle writer who was an
advertising copywriter in a former life. Her work has
appeared in The Gettysburg Review, New Letters, The
Louisville Review, Cold Mountain Review, River Teeth,
Chicago Quarterly Review and elsewhere. She is an avid
but cautious skier and enthusiastic world traveler.

Phil Goldstein
Phil Goldstein's first (and maybe best) story was written
when was 6 and concerned two pizza-shop owning
brothers who thwarted an alien invasion by cooking the
aliens in their pizza ovens. When he is not writing
professionally or personally he enjoys going on long
hikes with his wife and dog. He is a total nerd (Lord of
the Rings trivia is his forte) and is proud of that.

KJ Hannah Greenberg
KJ Hannah Greenberg tilts at social ills and encourages
personal evolutions via poetry, prose, and visual art. Her
images have appeared as interior art in many places,
including Foliate Oak Literary Magazine, Kissing
Dynamite, Les Femmes Folles, Mused, Piker Press, The
Academy of the Heart and Mind, The Front Porch
Review, and Yellow Mama and as cover art for
Impspired [sic], Pithead Chapel, Red Flag Poetry, Right
Hand Pointing, The Broken City, and Torah Tidbits.
Additionally, some of her digital paintings are featured
alongside of her poetry in One-Handed Pianist (Hekate
Publishing, 2021).

Steven Anthony George
Steven Anthony George is a resident of Fairmont, WV.
His poetry and short stories have been published in
several online and print journals, as well as the
anthologies Diner Stories: Off The Menu (2015) and
Twice Upon A Time: Fairytale, Folklore, & Myth.
Reimagined & Remastered (2015). He is n autistic adult
and active in the autism community. He often speaks and
has written on the topic of autism self-advocacy to
parents and teachers.

Joe Gianotti
Joe Gianotti hails from Whiting, Indiana, a Chicago
suburb and blue collar town. He teaches English at
Lowell High School, a job that he loves. Joe is a baseball
fan, loves to learn about geography, and owns an
extensive Funko Pop collection, which is on display in
his classroom.

John Grey
John Grey is an Australian poet, US resident, recently
published in Sheepshead Review, Poetry Salzburg
Review and Hollins Critic. Latest books, "Leaves On
Pages" "Memory Outside The Head" and "Guest Of
Myself" are available through Amazon. Work upcoming
in Ellipsis, Blueline and International Poetry Review.

Joel Harris
Joel Harris is a Trinidadian poet and artist who
constantly experiments. In 2020 he was shortlisted at
Into The Void's Poetry Prize. His work will appear in
Heavy Feather Review's #NoMorePresidents next year.
He leads counterradicalization workshops and training
programs with Sirius International Caribbean Defence
Contractors Ltd., the firm he co-founded.

Phil Huffy
Phil Huffy had a long career doing something else. He used to write boring stuff for his job. He enjoys cycling, camping out, small hikes, moonlight, and motor trips. Recently, he got an electric bike and has not been seen since.

Olivia Ivings
Olivia Ivings lives in Atlanta, Georgia, with her two dogs, Aurora and Matilda. She enjoys eating leftovers and acting like she knows what is going on (even though she doesn't). When she isn't walking with her dogs or dusting the leaves of her plants, you can find her sliding across the floor like a snake.

Mark Jackley
Mark Jackley's work has appeared in Fifth Wednesday, Sugar House Review, The Cape Rock, Natural Bridge, and other journals. HIs new book of poems Many Suns Will Rise is forthcoming from Main Street Rag Press. He lives in Purcellville, Virginia, in the foothills of the Blue Ridge Mountains.

Meghan Kemp-Gee
Meghan Kemp-Gee writes poetry, comics, and scripts of all kinds somewhere between Vancouver BC and Fredericton NB. She teaches composition and co-created the world's best comic about ultimate frisbee. You can find her on Twitter @MadMollGreen.

Jeffery Letterly
Jeffrey Letterly is a composer and multi-disciplined performer. He was born and raised in the heartland of the Midwest and now resides in Syracuse, NY. His poetry comes out of nowhere, which is somewhere that can be anywhere.

Kalyn Livernois
Kalyn Livernois is an MFA candidate at New England
College. She is a prose editor at Cobra Milk and the
managing editor of Variant Literature's journal. Her
work has most recently appeared in Emerge Literary
Journal, Anti-Heroin Chic, and The Dead Mule School
of Southern Literature. You can find her on Twitter
@kalynroseanne.

J.C Mari
J.C Mari resides in Florida. He's the author of the poetry
collection "the sun sets like faces fade right before you
pass out".

Corey Mesler
COREY MESLER, a Trappist Monk, was raised by
wolves. He has Canadian blood, which, unlike Canadian
Bacon, doesn't stay fresh if left out. He has rambled
around some, mostly from the bed to the bathroom, and
once saw Prince in the Los Angeles airport. He also
dated Vanity's sister, but has no claims to ethnic insider
information. He published some novels that some people
liked. As of this date, he has written 4,861 poems. He
also claims to have written "Green Acres." With his wife
he owns Burke's Book Store (est. 1875) in Memphis:
tells him which shirt goes with which pants.

Corey Miller
Corey Miller's writing has appeared in Booth, Pithead
Chapel, Atticus Review, Hobart, X-R-A-Y, and
elsewhere. He reads for TriQuarterly, Longleaf Review,
and Barren Magazine. When Corey isn't brewing beer
for a living in Cleveland, he likes to take the dogs for
adventures. Follow him on Twitter @IronBrewer or at
www.CoreyMillerWrites.com

Jay Mora-Shihadeh
Jay Mora-Shihadeh (He/Him) resides in Sarasota Fl with his wife and dog, Samuel. Jay's verse hounds him like his dog crying in the night. One day he woke up and decided to heed that call, and let the words flow. Today, he works at his craft every day, for better or worse, and most days you can find him beating around his blog- The Artist from the Inside Out
https://artistfromtheinsideout.wordpress.com/

Cyndy Muscatel
I have written features and humor for The Desert Sun, Desert Magazine, 92260, LQ Magazine, and Healthy Living. I have also written for many other publications including The Seattle Times, The Mercer Island Reporter, The Desert Post Weekly, Palm Canyon Times, and Westlake Magazine. A former high school English teacher, I now teach memoir writing in Kona, Hawaii, and I write a monthly column for Lake Sherwood Life magazine. My blogs, A Corner of My Mind and Writing Do's and Don'ts, are available at cyndymuscatel.blog.

Brontë Pearson
Brontë Pearson is a science journalist and creative writer from Oklahoma. Her essays, short stories, and poetry seek to expose the art of being human through natural discoveries of the body, environment, and mind. Her work has been published in numerous online and print publications and 'best of' anthologies, including Nonbinary Review, The Smart Set, Motherly, The Mighty, Arkansas's Best Emerging Poets, Door is a Jar Magazine, and others. Brontë is also a mother and an enthusiast of alternative rock music, dark chocolate, and cats.

Robert Pegel
Robert Pegel is a husband and father is a husband and
father whose only child, his son Calvin, died in 2016.
Calvin died in his sleep of unknown causes at age 16.
Robert writes to ponder life's mysteries. He tries to
transform his grief by creating. Robert graduated from
Columbia University where he majored in English. He
has been published in Trouvaille Review, Fahmidan
Journal, The Madrigal, ZiN Daily, The Remington
Review, Spirit Fire Review, The Rye Whiskey Review,
As Above So Below and others. He has work
forthcoming in Sledgehammer Lit, North Dakota
Quarterly and Resurrection Magazine. Robert lives in
Andover, NJ with his wife, Zulma and their Min Pin
dog, Chewy.

Scarlett Peterson
Scarlett Peterson is poet, essayist, and lesbian. She is
currently working on her PhD at Georgia State
University. She received her MFA at Georgia College.
Her work can be found in Moon City Review, The
Lavender Review, Cosmonauts Avenue, Peculiar,
Pidgeonholes, Gargoyle Magazine, Ponder Review,
Madcap Review, Counterclock Journal, The Shore,
Poetry Online, Skink Beat Review, Eunoia Review, and
more.

Vincent Antonio Rendoni
Vincent Antonio Rendoni (he / him) is a Seattle-based
writer. He is a 2022 Jack Straw Fellow and the winner of
Blue Earth Review's 2021 Annual Flash Fiction Contest.
He is a contributor to What They Leave Behind: A
Latinx Anthology. His work has appeared / will be
appearing in the Texas Review, Juked, Fiction
Southeast, Sky Island Journal, Cordite Poetry Review,
and more.

Kevin A. Risner
Kevin A. Risner is a product of Ohio. He is the author of
Do Us a Favor (Variant Literature, 2021). He loves
reading, running, and enjoying a nice scotch — not all at
the same time.

Matthew Schultz
Matthew Schultz: bassist, vegan, poet. What else could
be said?

Claire Scott
Claire Scott is a recently retired psychotherapist who is
enjoying having more time to write, take long walks and
try to stay ahead of the weeds. She is excited to be
spending more time with her five grandchildren who are
scattered over the country.

Beatriz Seelaender
Beatriz Seelaender is a Brazilian writer, although she
doesn't quite believe in national borders. Right now, she
is probably tired and grumpy. Her dog, Uli, is her utmost
muse.

Nora Smith
Nora Smith is a copy editor living in Pittsburgh. They
can most often be found glued to a book under a pile of
blankets, or chasing a poem idea down through the
woods.

Gina Stratos
Gina Stratos is a writer living in northern Nevada. She
enjoys collecting words, sipping buttery Chardonnay,
and cancelling plans with friends. Her work can be read
in Dark River Review, Door Is A Jar, The Meadow,
Rabid Oak, and Words & Whispers.

Edward Michael Supranowicz
Edward Michael Supranowicz is the grandson of Irish
and Russian/Ukrainian immigrants. He grew up on a
small farm in Appalachia. He has a grad background in
painting and printmaking. Some of his artwork has
recently or will soon appear in Fish Food, Streetlight,
Another Chicago Magazine, Door Is a Jar, The Phoenix,
and other journals. Edward is also a published poet.

w v sutra
w v sutra can be found writing poetry on his horse farm
in East Tennessee. His work has been published in
various outlets, and interested readers may amuse
themselves by seeking them out! He is easily identified
by his long braided beard.

Mary Grace van der Kroef
It's the simple things that sustain us, like a good cup of
coffee to dunk a cookie in. Or the bubbles from a cold
Dr. Peper that tickles the nose and forces a sneeze. But
most of all, holding another person's hand through time
and space as they read my poetry.

Alexandra Williams
Alexandra Williams is a UK-based freelance writer.
Born in London, she now lives in a village in Berkshire
where she tries to fit in with her green-fingered
neighbours by growing vegetables (with varying degrees
of success). She writes poetry and prose and, in her spare
time, enjoys walking (whilst thinking about poetry and
prose).

Bill Wolak
Bill Wolak is a poet, collage artist, and photographer
who has just published his eighteenth book of poetry
entitled All the Wind's Unfinished Kisses with Ekstasis

Editions. His collages and photographs have appeared as cover art for such magazines as Phoebe, Harbinger Asylum, Baldhip Magazine, Barfly Poetry Magazine, Ragazine, Cardinal Sins, Pithead Chapel, The Wire's Dream, Thirteen Ways Magazine, Phantom Kangaroo, Rathalla Review, Free Lit Magazine, The Magnolia Review, Typehouse Magazine, The Round, and Flare Magazine.

Fran Zell
I am the author of The Marcy Stories (Bottom Dog Press) which won the Banta Award for literary achievement from the Wisconsin Library Association. Other work, including fiction, theater reviews and journalism, has appeared in Mondoweiss.net, Splashmags.com, Other Voices, Playgirl Magazine, Chicago Reader, Madison (WI) Isthmus and Milwaukee Magazine. I am a former feature writer for the Chicago Tribune and a recipient of grants from the Illinois Arts Council and the Barbara Deming Memorial Fund, Money for Women.

Submission Guidelines

Door Is A Jar Magazine is looking for well-crafted poetry, fiction, nonfiction, drama and artwork for our print and digital publication. Please read over these submission guidelines carefully before submitting any work.

Our magazine features new artists and writers and works that are accessible for all readers. Please look at our current and archived issues before submitting your work. Works that are confusing, abstract, or unnecessarily fancy will not be considered.

We only accept new, unpublished work. If you have posted something to your website or social media, this counts as being published.

Contributors can submit to multiple categories; however, only submit once to each category until you have received our decision about your piece.

Upload your submissions to Submittable with the category you are submitting to and your first and last name as the filename. Within the cover letter please include your full name, contact info, and 3-sentence bio.

We accept simultaneous submissions; however, please notify us immediately if a piece is accepted elsewhere. We reserve first initial publishing rights and then all rights revert back to the author. We do not pay contributors at this time.

For more information please visit doorisajarmagazine.net

www.ingramcontent.com/pod-product-compliance
Lightning Source LLC
Chambersburg PA
CBHW052004220626
47052CB00004B/1089